DINK, JOSH, AND RUTH ROSE
AREN'T THE ONLY KID DETECTIVES!

WHAT ABOUT YOU?

CAN YOU FIND THE HIDDEN MESSAGE INSIDE THIS BOOK?

There are 26 illustrations in this book, not counting the one on the title page, the map at the beginning, or the picture of the cabins that repeats at the start of many of the chapters. In each of the 26 illustrations, there's a hidden letter. If you can find all the letters, you will spell out a secret message!

If you're stumped, the answer is on the bottom of page 133.

HAPPY DETECTING!

This book is dedicated to Mike Darby and his family.
—R.R.

To Molly and Jesse
—J.S.G.

Text copyright © 2006 by Ron Roy
Cover art copyright © 2015 by Stephen Gilpin
Interior illustrations copyright © 2006 by John Steven Gurney

All rights reserved. Published in the United States by Random House Children's Books, a division of Random House LLC, a Penguin Random House Company, New York. Originally published in paperback by Random House Children's Books, New York, in 2006.

Random House and the colophon and A to Z Mysteries are registered trademarks and A Stepping Stone Book and the colophon and the A to Z Mysteries colophon are trademarks of Random House LLC.

Visit us on the Web!
SteppingStonesBooks.com
randomhousekids.com

Educators and librarians, for a variety of teaching tools, visit us at RHTeachersLibrarians.com

Library of Congress Cataloging-in-Publication Data
Roy, Ron.
Detective Camp / by Ron Roy ; illustrated by John Steven Gurney.
p. cm. — (A to Z mysteries Super edition ; #1) "A Stepping Stone Book."
Summary: While learning detective skills at a sleep-away camp, Dink and his friends uncover a real mystery involving stolen paintings.
ISBN 978-0-375-83534-6 (trade) — ISBN 978-0-375-93534-3 (lib. bdg.) —
ISBN 978-0-307-49481-8 (ebook)
[1. Camps—Fiction. 2. Mystery and detective stories.] I. Gurney, John Steven, ill. II. Title. III. Series: Roy, Ron. A to Z mysteries Super edition ; #1.
PZ7.R8139 Dg 2006 [Fic]—dc22 2005016675

Printed in the United States of America
31

This book has been officially leveled by using the F&P Text Level Gradient™ Leveling System.

Random House Children's Books supports the First Amendment and celebrates the right to read.

SUPER EDITION 1

Detective
Camp

by Ron Roy

illustrated by
John Steven Gurney

A STEPPING STONE BOOK™

Random House 🏠 New York

CHAPTER 1

"Here y'are, kids," the taxi driver told Dink, Josh, and Ruth Rose. "Get out and stretch your legs and I'll fetch your luggage."

The kids stepped out of the taxi in Bear Walk, Vermont. They were standing next to a gravel driveway in front of an old lodge built of timber. A banner over the wide porch said WELCOME TO DETECTIVE CAMP.

Behind the lodge stood a red barn with its doors open wide.

Dink noticed a few picnic tables on the lawn between the lodge and the barn. Across from the driveway stood three log cabins surrounded by wildflowers, shrubs, and trees. Off to the side of the cabins stood a larger building. Dink noticed a sign that said WASH-HOUSE. White arrows pointed boys to one door and girls to another.

"Where are we supposed to sleep?" Josh asked. Like Dink, he wore cutoff jean shorts and a T-shirt.

"Didn't you read the letter?" Dink asked, winking at Ruth Rose. "Josh Pinto sleeps in a bear cave." Dink's full name was Donald David Duncan, but his friends called him Dink.

Josh didn't say anything, but he made a goofy face at Dink.

"In those cabins, I guess," said Ruth Rose, pointing. "I see some other kids over there." Ruth Rose liked to dress all in one color. Today she wore pink from her headband to her sneakers.

"Tell me again why we're in Bear Walk, Vermont," Josh said, glancing around. "I'll bet there are bears everywhere!"

"We came to Detective Camp because we love solving mysteries," Ruth Rose said. "Besides, none of us has been to sleepaway camp before. It'll be fun! We'll learn all about—"

"Yo!" someone yelled. The kids looked toward the cabins. Three teenagers were walking toward them. They each wore a white T-shirt with DETECTIVE CAMP on the front and green shorts. Whistles hung from lanyards around their necks.

"Are you the kids from Green Lawn, Connecticut?" a tall boy with a buzz cut asked.

"Yes," Dink said. "I'm Dink, and these

are my friends Josh and Ruth Rose."

"I'm Buzzy Steele," the boy said, smiling. "You two guys are in my cabin, the one with the moose over the door."

"And I'm Angie Doe," the girl said. She had red hair in pigtails. "Ruth Rose, you're in Fox Cabin with me. You'll have nine roommates!"

The other boy had broad shoulders and dark skin. "I'm Lucas Washington," he said. "Call me Luke. I have Bear Cabin with eight more guys."

"How many kids are here altogether?" Dink asked.

"Twenty-six," Angie said. "Sixteen boys and ten girls."

The taxi driver handed the kids' packs and sleeping bags to them. "Have a good time," he said, getting back into the taxi. Then he turned the cab around and pulled away.

"Let's get you kids into your cabins,"

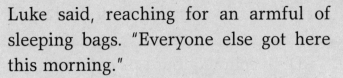

Luke said, reaching for an armful of sleeping bags. "Everyone else got here this morning."

They followed the three counselors onto the lawn. Stone paths led up to each of the three small porches.

"After you get unpacked, we're all meeting down by Shady Lake," Angie told the kids. "About twenty minutes, okay? Just follow that path, and the lake will be right in front of you. Ready to meet your cabinmates, Ruth Rose?"

"Yes!" Ruth Rose said. "See you later, guys." She followed Angie into a cabin with a wooden cutout of a fox over the door.

"Later," Luke said. He loped next door.

Buzzy led Dink and Josh through a door with a moose cutout over it. Inside the cabin, six boys were reading and playing board games. A shelf in one corner was overflowing with books and games.

Dink counted four sets of bunk beds. Near the door was a single bed. Dink assumed that was where Buzzy would sleep.

"Yo, guys, listen up!" Buzzy yelled.

"Come and meet Dink and Josh from Connecticut."

Six boys turned toward Dink and Josh. They smiled and, one by one, introduced themselves and shook hands.

Dink tried to remember the six new names and faces: A black-haired boy

named Billy Wong. A thin kid with braces called Hunter. Ian and Brendan, twins with blond hair so light it appeared white. Duke, a tall boy. And Campbell, a short blond kid with a big smile.

"If you need to wash up or use the bathroom, that's all in the big building on the other side of Fox Cabin," Buzzy told the boys.

"We have to go outside to the bathroom?" Josh asked.

Buzzy nodded. "Yep. The showers are there, too," he said. "And don't let the hot water run too long, or someone gets a cold shower! You all need to be down at Shady Lake in about ten minutes, okay?"

"Are we going swimming?" Hunter asked. "Are there snakes in the water?"

"No and yes," Buzzy said, grinning. "There are a few harmless water snakes, but we're not going swimming today. We're just having a meeting with all the other campers."

Dink and Josh headed for the only set of bunks not piled up with the other kids' stuff.

"I guess this one is ours," Dink said. "Top or bottom?"

"Top," Josh said, tossing his sleeping bag up onto the mattress. "That way, if a bear comes in, he gets you first."

Dink grinned. "Bears can climb, Josh," he said.

"I'll still take the top bunk," Josh said. He grabbed his backpack and climbed the ladder.

Dink unrolled his sleeping bag and fluffed up the pillow he found on his mattress. As he emptied his backpack, he glanced out the window just over his bed. He could see a wooden fence separating the lawn from deep woods.

He arranged his clothes in a cubby that already had his name on it. He set his toothbrush and other toilet articles on the windowsill. He'd brought a couple of books, which he stood next to his toothpaste. The titles were *Wild Animals of Vermont* and *Danny Doon, Boy Detective.*

Josh was on top, wrestling with his sleeping bag.

"Are you ready?" Dink asked.

"Almost," Josh said. "My brothers used this sleeping bag last, and they tied about a million knots in the string."

"Okay, let's hustle," Buzzy called out. "Moose Cabin is never late! Now let's go, little moosies!"

The other six boys stampeded out the cabin door and raced for the path that led to the lake. A minute later, Buzzy followed them.

Dink waited for Josh on the porch.

Josh snuck up behind Dink and said, "Come back inside. I want to show you something."

"What?" Dink said as he followed Josh. "Come on, we're gonna be late on our first day!"

"Look," Josh said. He was pointing to a small wooden chest under Buzzy's bed. It had a hasp, and the padlock was in the locked position.

"Josh, what do I care if—"

"After the other kids left, I saw Buzzy hide something in there," Josh said. "He was real careful, like he didn't want anyone to see what he was doing."

"But Josh the snoop saw him, right?" Dink asked.

Josh nodded. "This is Detective Camp, right?" he said. "Well, I'm being a detective!"

CHAPTER 2

Dink and Josh ran down the path. A couple of minutes later, they heard voices and followed them to the lake.

They found all the other kids sitting on tree stumps arranged in a big circle. In the center was a ring of rocks surrounding a pile of wood. A few yards away, a dock jutted out into the lake. There were several canoes piled upside down on the dock. Paddles stuck out from beneath each canoe.

Ruth Rose had saved two stumps, so Dink and Josh sat on either side of her.

"You two are late," Ruth Rose said in

a whisper. "Bad Moose boys!"

Suddenly a loud whistle pierced the air. Angie was standing on a stump with her whistle in her mouth.

"Welcome to Detective Camp!" she said. "Whenever you hear a whistle like this, you need to stop what you're doing and listen. Later, you'll be getting daily schedules. For now, the guys and I want to tell you what to expect over the next week."

She turned and pointed toward the dock. "No one is allowed on the dock or near the canoes unless you're with a counselor," Angie went on. "You'll get a chance to swim or canoe every day, starting tomorrow."

Luke took over next. "Each day, you'll also get a chance to do other camp activities like crafts, nature walks, stuff like that," he said. "You'll also learn detective skills from a real detective!"

A lot of the kids whistled and clapped at the word *detective.*

"You're expected to do camp chores, too," Luke continued.

"What kind of chores?" a girl with a long ponytail asked. "Like dishes and stuff?"

"No dishes, Jade, but you're expected to keep your bunks neat," Angie said. "And we sweep the cabins every day. Some of you may want to feed the chickens and collect eggs. We even have a vegetable garden, if you like getting your hands dirty. Anyway, the chores don't take long, and you can switch around so no one gets bored."

"When do we eat?" Josh asked, getting a laugh.

"Mealtimes are sacred around here," Buzzy said. "Mario is the cook, and he won't wait for latecomers. Breakfast is at eight, lunch at noon, and supper is promptly at five o'clock."

"We eat outside on the picnic tables by the barn, unless the weather is bad," Angie added. "If it rains, we don't eat."

Most of the kids went silent and stared at her.

"Are you kidding?" Josh asked.

Angie grinned. "Yes. We eat in the barn if it rains. So that's another chore, to help carry the picnic tables inside if the weather looks bad."

"When you're not doing these camp things, you'll have free time to relax, write letters home, whatever," Luke said. "Okay, any more questions?"

"Wait, Luke," Buzzy said. "We forgot to tell them the most important thing!"

"Oh yeah, what's that?" Luke asked with a big grin on his face.

"The Marvelous Mystery Map!" Buzzy said. "Detective Robb will explain it all later. For now, we just want to clue you in that there'll be a treasure hunt with a really cool prize."

"Awesome!" a bunch of kids yelled.

"One more thing before we head up to the barn," Angie said. "This'll be fun. Break up into your three cabin groups. We want each group to decide on a cabin cheer. Try to keep it under fifteen words. Later, each cabin will get to yell out their cheer. Okay, get busy. You've got ten minutes!"

The kids all scrambled around to sit with their cabinmates. Dink and Josh and the other six boys from Moose Cabin sat under a shady pine tree.

"This is so cool!" Hunter said. "I've never been to camp before!"

"Does anyone have any ideas for a cheer?" asked Billy.

"How about putting in something that rhymes with *moose*?" said Ian, one of the twins.

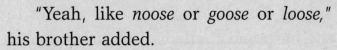

"Yeah, like *noose* or *goose* or *loose*," his brother added.

"Or *juice*," said Josh.

"Or *caboose*," added Campbell.

"What about this?" Dink said. "HEY, I AM A MOOSE. I DRINK MY JUICE. AT NIGHT, I SLEEP IN MY CABOOSE."

"That's sixteen words," Duke said.

"I have an idea," Campbell said. "MOOSIES ROCK! MOOSIES ROLL! MOOSIES RULE!"

"I like that better than mine," Dink said.

"Everyone else does, too," Josh said, grinning at Dink. "Let's take a vote. If you like Campbell's idea, raise your hand!"

Eight hands flew into the air.

"Okay, time's up, everyone," Angie announced a few minutes later. "If you didn't finish, you'll have time to get together with your cabinmates before supper tonight. Now we'll head over to the barn and the lodge so you can meet the Darbys."

In a long, straggling line, the kids followed the three counselors back along the path.

"Did your cabin finish making a cheer?" Dink asked Ruth Rose.

"No," Ruth Rose said. "But we have some good ideas."

"We did our cheer," Dink said.

"You did? Tell me!" Ruth Rose begged.

Both boys shook their heads.

"You'll have to wait," Josh teased.

The group went around the lodge to the barn. It was bigger than Dink had thought when he first saw it. There was a long extension in the back. Through the open doors, Dink could see archery equipment hanging on one wall. There was a big empty space in the middle of the barn floor, and in a corner sat three potter's wheels and shelves holding craft supplies.

"Okay, campers, gather around," Buzzy yelled. "This is where you'll come for any craft activities. We eat on those picnic tables over there. Around the side is the chicken coop and Mote's house."

"Whose house?" one of the girls asked.

"Remote is a goat," Buzzy said. "He's the camp mascot. He once chewed up the Darbys' TV remote. Since then, everyone calls him Remote, but I call him Mote the goat."

Suddenly a large red rooster strutted around the side of the barn. He had red and black feathers and a fierce-looking beak. He stopped when he saw all the strangers.

"And this is Ronald the rooster," Luke said. "He and Remote are buddies, but he's not very friendly with anyone else. So watch out!"

Ignoring everyone, Ronald began scratching the ground for bugs and worms.

"Next we're going into the lodge," Angie continued. "The Darbys are excited to meet you. Remember, this is their home. They love reading mystery and detective stories, so they decided to create this camp.

"This is its first year, so it's sort of an experiment. They hope to have even more kids here next summer."

Buzzy held the back door open and everyone filed into the lodge. They walked into a large, bright kitchen. A tall man wearing an apron was standing at a worktable, chopping vegetables.

"Hi, I'm Mario," the man said. "I do all the cooking, so be nice to me! And on your way out, grab a cookie. I'm

taking a batch out of the oven in three minutes."

Mario's head was completely bald, and he wore a red bandanna as a headband. He had a large brown mustache that curled up into pointy ends.

"Thanks, Mario!" everyone said.

"Let's go into the great room," Angie said, passing through a doorway.

They all gathered in a huge room filled with sofas, tables, lamps, and more books than a small library. Most of the walls had bookcases, and they were all stuffed.

Several paintings hung on the walls. Some were so old and dirty that Dink couldn't tell what he was looking at. But others were bright and clean, as if they'd just been painted.

Dink noticed Buzzy peering into a cabinet with glass doors. On the shelves inside were dozens of small animal figurines. They were metal and gleamed softly like the silver teapot Dink's mom used only on holidays.

Just then they all heard a screeching noise. A door slid open, revealing an elevator. As all the kids stared, a man and a woman walked slowly off the elevator. They both had white hair and wore glasses. The woman used a walker.

Their wrinkled faces lit up when they saw the gang of kids.

"Hello," the man said. "I am Michael Darby. This is my wife, Bessie. Welcome to our home!"

The couple walked among the campers, shaking hands.

"I'll try to remember your names, but forgive an old lady if I forget!" Bessie said.

"Oh, excuse me," another voice said from behind the group.

They turned and saw a woman coming down the central stairs. Her black dress matched her hair, and she wore rose-colored glasses. She rested one pale hand on the banister as she paused at the bottom of the stairs.

Dink thought he'd never seen such white skin before. Then he realized the woman was wearing white rubber gloves.

"I am Mademoiselle Musée," the woman said.

CHAPTER 3

"Mademoiselle is living in Darby Lodge while she cleans our poor old paintings," Bessie Darby said. "How are they coming, my dear?"

The woman bowed slightly. "Very well, Mrs. Darby," she said with a French accent. "Only a few more, and then I will be gone and you will have your dining room back again."

"May we watch you clean a painting?" Ruth Rose asked.

"Perhaps," Mademoiselle Musée said. "If you have some free time later, come to visit me, yes? Mr. and Mrs. Darby, do you have a moment?"

"Of course, Mademoiselle," Mr. Darby said.

"Okay, gang, let's get some of Mario's cookies," Luke said, heading back toward the kitchen.

As Dink followed, he noticed that Buzzy was no longer in the group. Shrugging, Dink kept walking. As he entered the kitchen, he smelled something wonderful, and his mouth began to water.

Mario stood by his worktable, smiling. In front of him was a platter piled high with warm cookies.

"One to a customer," Mario said. He twirled the ends of his mustache and wiggled his dark eyebrows. Everyone laughed and took a cookie as they filed past.

Outside again, the kids sat at the picnic tables and ate their cookies. Suddenly a white and brown goat shot around the corner of the barn. He had a beard, short horns, and pointy black hooves. Ronald the rooster was perched on the goat's back, flapping his wings.

"Everyone, this is Remote!" Angie said. "I think he wants a cookie. Watch this."

The kids all stood up as Remote— with Ronald on his back—approached the kitchen door. He butted the door with his head. A few seconds later, Mario appeared with a cookie in his hand. He gave a small piece to Ronald and fed the rest to the goat.

"Awesome!" Josh said.

"Okay, kids, there's an hour left before supper," Luke said. "If you're not unpacked, that would be a good way to spend the time. If your cabin needs more time coming up with your cheer, you can do that. We'll all meet here at five o'clock."

"What do you want to do?" Josh asked Dink and Ruth Rose.

"Fox Cabin is having a meeting to finish our cheer," Ruth Rose said. "If we get through before five, I'll look for you guys." She got up and joined a bunch of girls at another table.

"Why don't we go exploring?" Dink asked Josh. "There's woods behind the cabins."

Dink and Josh headed for the cabins, then walked around toward the back. "Wait a sec," Josh said. "I want to grab my sketchbook."

They climbed the steps to the porch

and pushed open the screen door.

Buzzy Steele was kneeling on the floor next to one of the bunk beds. He jumped up when he heard Dink and Josh come in. Looking embarrassed, Buzzy moved toward his own bed.

"I dropped my pen," Buzzy said. "It

rolled under Hunter's bed."

Buzzy lifted some papers off his own bed and showed them to Dink and Josh. "These are the daily schedules. You guys want to tack one to the door? I'll bring the others over to Angie and Luke."

Handing Dink the paper and a thumbtack, Buzzy left the cabin.

"That was weird," Josh said after Buzzy had gone.

Dink glanced at the schedule. "What?" he asked.

"Buzzy snooping around in here, that's what," Josh said.

"Josh, he wasn't snooping," Dink said. "He lives in this cabin, and he was getting his pen. You're the snoop."

"Yeah, so where is this pen he said rolled under the bed?" Josh asked. "He wasn't carrying it when he left."

"Come on, we only have forty-five minutes," Dink said. "Let's go see what dangerous animals are sleeping behind our cabin."

At five o'clock, all twenty-six kids were seated at the picnic tables by the barn. Angie, Luke, and Buzzy carried platters of food and pitchers of milk to the three tables. Everyone chattered as the food came out.

Buzzy stood on his bench and blew his whistle. All eyes turned to him.

"Hi, guys," he said. "I hope you're ready with your cheers. Let's have one now, one before dessert, and one down at Shady Lake later. Okay, who wants to be first?"

"Moose Cabin!" yelled Campbell. The eight boys from Moose Cabin stood up and made a circle.

"MOOSIES ROCK! MOOSIES ROLL! MOOSIES RULE!" they all shouted.

Everyone else clapped or whistled.

"That was great," Luke said. "Okay, let's eat!" They all began passing platters of hamburgers and rolls.

Suddenly a scream came from the kitchen. Before anyone could react, the door flew open and Mademoiselle Musée rushed outside. "My ring!" she cried. "It is gone. I left it on my work-table, and it has vanished!"

Mario came up behind the upset woman. "We can search," he told her.

"Could you have left it somewhere else, maybe on the sink when you washed your hands?"

"No!" Mademoiselle insisted. "It was on my table in the dining room. I take it off because the stone cuts the rubber gloves I wear. I put it there this morning!"

Every kid stared at her.

"My—my parents gave me that ring," Mademoiselle Musée wailed. "I've had it since I was a little girl." Then she turned and walked back into the lodge, wringing her hands.

Dink looked at Josh, who nodded and raised his eyebrows. Dink knew then that Josh was thinking the same thing he was: could the missing ring be hidden in Buzzy Steele's locked chest?

"Come on, guys, let's finish our supper," Angie said. "I'm sure the ring will turn up somewhere."

Just then the goat came around a corner. He sniffed the air, then trotted up to Dink's table with his mouth open.

"Maybe the *goat* took the ring!" one of the girls cried. "Last summer, my cousin's goat ate his watch!"

"How could Remote get in the lodge?" one of the Bear Cabin boys asked.

"Him? He sneaks in all the time," Mario said. "The lock on this door hasn't worked in years. He just butts it open. I have to keep the food up high so he doesn't steal it all."

"I'll call a vet later," Luke said. "Maybe we can get Remote x-rayed!"

When Dink looked up, Josh was staring at him. He was slowly shaking his head back and forth.

A few kids began talking, and the tension slowly drifted away.

"Okay, who wants to do a cheer

next?" Buzzy called out. They had finished the burgers and were waiting for dessert.

"We will," one of the girls answered.

The ten girls made a long line across the lawn. Then they split into three groups. Ruth Rose and Jade made up the first group. The next group had three girls, and there were five in the last.

All ten girls stood straight, facing the picnic tables. Suddenly they all moved at the same time, changing their bodies into different shapes.

At first, no one could figure out what the shapes were supposed to be. Each girl looked different as they all bent their backs, arms, and legs.

Then one of the boys from Bear Cabin yelled, "I know! They made letters. It spells out GO, FOX CABIN!"

Then everyone else saw it, and they all began to cheer, "Go, Fox!"

"That was terrific," Angie said. "It was the best silent cheer I've ever seen! Now let's have ice cream!"

Luke and Buzzy brought tubs of ice cream from the kitchen. They went around the tables scooping vanilla or chocolate into bowls.

"Save room for s'mores later!" Angie called out.

"While you're eating, I'll read you tomorrow's schedule," Luke said.

He read from a sheet:

"7:00—RISE AND SHINE

8:00—BREAKFAST

9:00—STRAIGHTEN BUNKS AND TIDY CABIN

9:30—MARVELOUS MYSTERY MAP TREASURE HUNT

10:30—DETECTIVE SKILLS WITH DETECTIVE ROBB

12:00—LUNCH

1:00—REST, WRITE LETTERS

1:30—CAMP ACTIVITIES. This is when you get to swim or do archery and stuff.

3:00—AFTERNOON CHORES
4:00—FREE TIME
5:00—SUPPER
6:00—CAMPFIRE
8:30—QUIET TIME IN CABINS
9:00—IN BED
9:15—LIGHTS OUT."

"How will we remember all that?" Ian called out.

"You'll find a copy of the schedule tacked to your cabin door," Buzzy said. "Now who's ready for a campfire by the lake?"

CHAPTER 4

"Do you think someone really stole Mademoiselle Musée's ring?" Ruth Rose whispered to Dink and Josh. They were hiking toward the lake.

"I do," Josh said. "And I have a good idea who."

"Josh thinks Buzzy Steele did it, right, Josh?" Dink said.

"Buzzy? Why?" asked Ruth Rose.

"He was sneaking around in our cabin," Josh said.

Dink shook his head. "He wasn't sneaking, Josh. He lives there, remember?" he said.

"Is anyone in your cabin missing anything?" asked Ruth Rose.

"Not yet," Josh said. "But I'm keeping my eye on him."

At the lake, kids were already sitting on the circle of tree stumps.

"Let's sit together," Dink said.

They found three open stumps and sat. Luke and Angie were crouched by the ring of rocks, lighting a fire under the wood. Minutes later, a nice little blaze was going.

Dink took a deep whiff of the burning wood. It smelled great. The sun was behind the trees and long shadows snaked along the beach. A few early fireflies were blinking among the tree branches.

"Okay, let's hear the Bear Cabin cheer!" Angie said. "Then we'll make s'mores!"

Everyone cheered as the eight boys

from Bear Cabin stood up and formed a circle. They threw their arms around each other's shoulders and put their heads together like football players in a huddle.

They began to chant:

"WE'RE THE BEARS! WHO CARES ABOUT BEARS? WE DO! WE DO! WE DO! BEAR CABIN! BEAR CABIN! BEAR CABIN!"

All the rest of the kids cheered, stomping their feet in the sand.

"I know that was more than fifteen words," one of the Bear boys said. "But the girls didn't use any words, so we borrowed a few of theirs!"

"Great job, guys," Buzzy said. He and Luke passed out graham crackers, marshmallows, and flat chocolate bars. Angie gave each kid a stick with a pointy end.

"In case you've never made a s'more before, listen up," Angie said. "First, break a cracker in two pieces and put a hunk of chocolate on one half. Then roast your marshmallow. When it's golden and a little mushy on the stick, plop it on the chocolate and slap the other half of the cracker on top. It's delicious!"

The kids took turns roasting their marshmallows. Pretty soon everyone had sticky lips and fingers. Instead of sitting on their stumps, a lot of the campers were lying in the sand, gazing into the fire. The sky had grown dark, and the stars were bright over their heads.

"While you kids are digesting your s'mores, we'll tell you about the Marvelous Mystery Map," Angie said. "You'll be meeting Detective Robb at breakfast tomorrow. He drew a map that leads to a special treasure, then he ripped the map into twenty-six pieces. Luke, Buzzy, and I hid them all over the camp. Each of you has to find one piece."

"How do we do that?" asked Josh.

"Alphabet clues," Luke said. "Buzzy, Angie, and I wrote the letters of the alphabet on twenty-six cards. Each of the map pieces will be found in a place that begins with a certain letter. To help you out, we put a clue on the back of each card. You'll each pick a card out of a hat tomorrow."

"I don't get it," Campbell said.

"Okay, here's an example," said Buzzy. "Suppose your card has the letter *W* on the front and a piece of bark taped to the back. Where would you go to look?"

"I'd go to the woodpile!" said Ruth Rose.

"And you'd be right!" Buzzy said.

"Cool!" Campbell said. "It's a treasure hunt!"

"You'll work in teams," Angie went on. "There are twenty-six of you, and you should form into teams of three or four kids. Remember, your goal is to find all twenty-six pieces of the map and put them back together. The treasure's location will be on the map."

"When do we start?" asked one of the girls.

"It's on your daily schedule," Angie said. "At nine-thirty, right after your morning chores, come up to the picnic tables to get your clue cards."

Suddenly Luke jumped on his stump with a banjo in his hands. "Who knows 'The Washerwoman Song'?" he yelled.

No one answered.

"Well, we do!" said Luke. "Come on, Angie and Buzzy, let's teach it to them."

While Luke plucked the banjo strings, all three sang:

"Way down south, in a wild, wet place,
There's a wishy-washy washer-woman washing her face.
Here's how the washerwoman washes her face.
She waves her arms all over the place.
She wiggles her rear
and pulls her ear.
She shakes her toes
and scratches her nose.

And that's how the washer-woman washes her face!"

"Now everyone stand up and try it," Luke said. "You have to make all the motions. Anyone who laughs has to sit down, and the last person standing is the winner!"

Luke started them off with his banjo. "Now sing, *'Way down south, in a wild, wet place . . .'"*

All twenty-six kids started singing. Within five seconds, they were all laughing and falling in the sand.

"I guess it's a tie," Luke said, grinning. "Tomorrow night, one of you can choose a song. Now let's put the fire out and head back."

"Not so fast!" Buzzy said with a big grin on his face. "Angie, tell the kids about the Shady Lake Monster."

"Oh, they don't want to hear about

the Shady Lake Monster!" Angie said, smiling at Buzzy.

"YES WE DO!" twenty-six kids screamed.

"Oh, all right," Angie said.

It was very dark now, and cooler. The kids leaned closer to the fire. They got quiet as Angie began speaking.

"Long, long ago, a forest ranger was camping near this very lake in July. The next morning, other rangers found just his hat. The man was never seen again. The following year, again in July, another person disappeared from the banks of Shady Lake." Angie pointed out at the dark water.

"This went on year in, year out. Every July, a person walking near this lake would disappear, never to be heard from again. Sometimes adults disappeared; sometimes it was children. Two years ago, a whole bunch of kids disappeared while camping here!"

Josh moaned, and someone else giggled in the dark.

"Anyway," Angie continued, "no one disappeared last July, so some people think the monster is gone. Of course, I have my own theory."

Angie leaned closer and whispered, "I think the monster is at the bottom of Shady Lake, hibernating. And while he's down there hibernating, he's getting very, very hungry! So keep your eyes open, especially when the sun goes down, just like . . . *now!*"

Suddenly everyone heard a huge splash in the lake.

"It's the monster!" Angie yelled.

The kids all screamed and jumped up. They tripped over their stumps, bumped into each other, and fell in the sand.

"Run for the cabins!" Buzzy yelled, barely able to keep from laughing.

The kids shrieked and tore away from the campfire. Dink and Josh burst into their cabin and jumped into their bunks. They were followed by the six other boys, laughing and growling like monsters.

"That was so cool," Campbell said. "But my uncle Mickey told me that same story about the camp he went to. He said he heard it from his camp counselors when he was a kid! Buzzy, Angie, and Luke are having a good laugh down there now."

"But what made that splash?" Josh asked.

"One of the counselors probably slipped away from the campfire in the dark," Campbell said. "When Angie said 'now!' Luke or Buzzy must have thrown a rock in the lake."

As soon as Dink's heartbeat had quieted down, he grabbed his toothbrush and headed for the washhouse.

When he returned to his bunk, Josh was at his cubby, pushing things aside to find his own toothbrush.

Dink kicked off his sneakers and flopped down on his bed. He picked up his Vermont book and began reading about white-tailed deer.

Dink heard a scratching sound outside his window. When he turned, he saw Ruth Rose peering in through the screen.

"What're you doing out there?" Dink asked.

"I found it!" Ruth Rose said. "Meet me around front under that big tree!"

"You found what?" Dink asked.

Ruth Rose put her hand near the screen. With the light spilling outside, Dink saw it clearly.

Resting in the palm of Ruth Rose's hand was a woman's ring.

CHAPTER 5

Dink grabbed Josh and pulled him out onto the cabin porch.

"What's going on?" Josh asked. "I haven't even brushed—"

"Ruth Rose found the ring," Dink whispered as he tugged Josh off toward the trees.

Ruth Rose joined them, scurrying from behind their cabin. "It was hidden under my mattress," she whispered. She showed the ring to Dink and Josh.

"Do you think it's hers?" Josh asked. "I mean Mad . . . what's her name."

"Mademoiselle Musée," Ruth Rose

said. "It must be, unless someone else is missing a ring."

"How did you find it?" Dink asked.

"My mattress was crooked," she said. "When I straightened it out, I felt the ring."

"So someone hid it there," Dink said. "But why?"

"I hate to say it, but maybe one of my cabinmates stole the ring," Ruth Rose said. "And maybe they hid it in case Mademoiselle Musée decided to search the cabins."

"If she did, she'd find the ring under your mattress and blame you for stealing it," Josh said.

Ruth Rose nodded. "I know," she said.

Josh chuckled. "At least we know Remote the goat didn't eat it," he said.

"What should we do?" Ruth Rose asked.

"Maybe we should tell the Darbys," Josh said.

"No, they'd just get all upset if they thought one of their campers was a thief," Ruth Rose said.

"Should we give it back to Mademoiselle tomorrow?" Dink asked. "Explain how you found it under your—"

"No," Ruth Rose interrupted, shaking her head. "Because then she'd go and upset the Darbys."

Just then Buzzy, Angie, and Luke came strolling toward the cabins, laughing and whispering. Ruth Rose pulled Dink and Josh farther into the shadows.

"I have an idea," she said. "Let's sneak into the lodge later and leave the ring where Mademoiselle Musée will be sure to find it in the morning."

Both boys stared at her.

"She'll just think she misplaced it," Ruth Rose went on.

"I guess that is the best thing to do," Dink said. "How will we get in? The doors might be locked."

"The kitchen door isn't," Josh said. "It doesn't lock. Remember how Mario told us the goat gets in?"

"Okay, set your watch alarm," Ruth Rose told Dink. She shoved the ring deep into the pocket of her shorts. "Meet right here at midnight!"

They split up, and Dink and Josh hurried into Moose Cabin.

"What's up, guys?" asked Buzzy. "It's time to get ready for bed."

"We were just talking to our friend Ruth Rose," Dink said.

"Okay, fellas, you can read or whatever for ten more minutes, then lights out," Buzzy said. "Sleep tight and don't let the Shady Lake Monster bite!"

Most of the kids laughed.

Josh got undressed and climbed up

the ladder to the top bunk.

Dink did the same, pulling on blue pajamas. He set the alarm on his watch, then tried to read. He was reading about bobcats, but all he could picture was someone hiding a stolen ring under Ruth Rose's mattress.

Later, after the lights were out, he kept thinking about that ring. For some reason, he didn't believe one of the girls in Fox Cabin was the thief. Could it be Buzzy? In his mind, Dink kept seeing the Moose Cabin counselor on his knees next to Hunter's bed.

Something *very* weird was going on in Detective Camp!

Dink was dreaming. He was riding Remote the goat through the forest, with Ronald the rooster on his shoulder. Ronald began to chirp in his ear, and Dink woke up.

The chirping was his watch. He fumbled for the tiny button to shut the alarm off. Midnight. Sitting up, Dink listened to the cabin noises. He heard a lot of soft breathing and a couple of deeper snores from Buzzy's bed.

Dink reached one leg up and kicked the top bunk to wake Josh. A moment later, Josh climbed down his ladder and stood next to Dink's bed.

Dink put a finger to his lips, and the two boys slipped out of the cabin. They hurried off the porch toward the trees.

They were both in pajamas and barefoot. The damp grass tickled the bottoms of Dink's feet. The moon was only partly visible through the trees, but it cast a glow on the ground and cabins.

"She'd better show up soon," Josh grumbled when they were deep in the shadows.

"I'm riiiight behind youuuu," Ruth

Rose said in a raspy voice.

Josh jumped and put his hand on his chest.

"Why don't you give me a heart attack!" he hissed.

Ruth Rose grinned. "Gee, are Moose Cabin boys afraid of the dark?" she asked.

"No, but I owe you one scare," Josh said. "Okay, are we gonna do this?"

The three of them hurried across the lawn, then the driveway. They crept past the picnic tables to the lodge's back door.

Dink looked for lights, but the windows were totally dark. He reached for the doorknob when Josh's hand stopped him.

"What if there's an alarm?" Josh asked.

Dink thought about all those paintings inside and that collection of animals that looked like valuable silver. "There could be, I guess," he said, pulling back his hand.

"Guys, if the Darbys didn't fix their broken lock, they sure wouldn't bother with an alarm," Ruth Rose said. She turned the doorknob and the door opened.

Dink felt his heart suddenly begin racing as they stepped into the dark kitchen. He crossed his fingers, hoping the Darbys were sound sleepers.

Then he remembered that Mademoiselle Musée also slept in the house. He crossed more fingers.

"This way," Ruth Rose whispered.

They walked around the long worktable, then through the swinging door into the dining room.

Moonlight shone through the windows, revealing a dining room table. On one end, a large towel covered a bunch of lumpy objects. Dink lifted the towel. He found bottles of liquid, some cotton balls, a package of Q-tips, and a small painting out of its frame. Even in the dim room, Dink could tell that the painting had been cleaned.

Dink replaced the towel carefully. At the far end of the room, he noticed a trunk. It stood on its end with the lid open sideways, like a door. Arranged on narrow shelves inside the trunk were brushes, more bottles, pliers, a hammer, and a few books. The binding on the biggest book read *100 Years of American Painters.*

Josh was staring up at a massive moose head over the fireplace mantel. "He looks like you, Dink," Josh said. "Same ears."

"Guys, look," Ruth Rose whispered. She was pointing to a small cardboard box. On its sides were the words: ALL-SAFE LATEX GLOVES.

"She wears these gloves," Ruth Rose said. "Why don't I leave her ring on the box? She'll have to notice it tomorrow."

Dink nodded. "Good idea," he said. "Now let's get out of here before Josh trips over something and the cops catch us for burglarizing!"

Ruth Rose carefully placed the ring on top of the box. The kids hurried out of the lodge and raced across the lawn toward the cabins. Angie and Buzzy were standing on the Moose Cabin porch. They didn't look happy.

"Uh-oh," Josh murmured. "Busted."

"Where have you kids been?" Angie asked.

Dink didn't know what to say. Josh opened his mouth like a goldfish gulping for oxygen.

"I found Mademoiselle's ring," Ruth Rose finally admitted. "We were just returning it. I left it on her worktable."

Both of the counselors stared at her.

"I found the ring under my mattress," Ruth Rose went on. "Dink and Josh and I didn't know what else to do, so we brought it to the dining room."

"The ring was under your mattress?" Angie said.

Ruth Rose nodded. "I don't know how it got there, honest!"

"You should have told one of us," Buzzy said. "We don't want you kids wandering around in the middle—"

"Ruth Rose, thank you for telling us," Angie broke in. "We'll take it from here. Now let's all get some sleep. Good night, everyone."

She and Ruth Rose went next door to Fox Cabin. Dink and Josh followed Buzzy inside. "No more midnight rambles, guys," Buzzy whispered as he slid under his covers.

Dink crawled into his sleeping bag.

As he was pulling it up to his chin, the moonlight fell on one of his pajama sleeves. He noticed something yellow on the cuff. It looked like a paint smudge.

Dink touched the smudge, and some of the yellow came off on his finger. It definitely looked like paint. And it was still sticky.

Where had he rubbed against wet paint? Then he remembered the painting on the table in the lodge dining room.

"Oh no," he muttered to himself as he closed his eyes. He hoped he hadn't damaged the painting.

As he fell asleep, he pictured himself being sued for a million dollars for ruining a masterpiece.

CHAPTER 6

A raucous scream brought Dink out of a deep sleep. He bolted up off his pillow. Through sleepy, startled eyes, Dink peered out the window over his bed.

Ronald was sitting on a fence post. The rooster flapped his wings and crowed once again. "COCK-A-DOODLE-DOO!"

Dink yawned, checked his watch, and saw that it was a little after five-thirty. He noticed the small yellow paint smear on his pajama cuff again. He unzipped his sleeping bag and looked around the cabin. Everyone else was still sound asleep. Buzzy was snoring loudly, with his mouth open.

Dink dressed quickly, put on sneakers, and left the cabin. A few stars still shone, although a dawn-pink glow was appearing through the trees.

He hurried across the dewy lawn to the back of the lodge. Opening the kitchen door quietly, he peered inside. No Mario. No anyone. He stepped inside and tiptoed to the dining room.

The first thing he checked was the box of gloves. The ring was still there, exactly where Ruth Rose had left it. Then he removed the towel and looked at the painting. Now he could see that it was a winter scene on a farm.

He peered closely at a yellow house. He figured that was where his pajama sleeve had picked up paint. The house looked fine, so he hadn't ruined it.

Gently, he placed a fingertip on the house—the paint was dry.

He replaced the towel, feeling better. He let himself out of the lodge and nearly bumped into Remote.

"What're you doing here?" Dink asked.

The goat playfully butted his head against Dink's leg.

"Sorry, no cookies," Dink said, giving the goat's head a rub.

Remote turned away and trotted toward one side of the barn. Dink followed him. They came to a small chicken coop enclosed by a wire fence. Dink could hear low clucking sounds, and he could definitely smell chicken manure!

Next to the henhouse stood a large doghouse with straw spilling out the door. Remote stepped inside and gracefully lay down with all four hooves tucked beneath his body.

"Okay, you go back to sleep," Dink said. "We don't eat till eight o'clock."

Just then Dink heard someone approaching on the gravel driveway. He walked around the barn and saw Mario stepping down from a black truck.

Dink stood still, feeling as if he'd been caught doing something wrong.

Mario walked toward the kitchen door, yawning. He saw Dink and stopped. "Early bird, eh?" he said.

"Ronald woke me up," Dink said. "I decided to look around."

"Want to help?" Mario asked. "Can you gather some eggs? There's a basket inside the coop."

"Sure," Dink said. "Um, do chickens bite?"

Mario laughed. "They might peck, but only if they're scared. Talk to them gently so they know you're not an enemy. If they're on a nest, just move your hand under them slowly and get the eggs."

Dink opened the coop door. He saw about a dozen chickens, all on nests built along one wall. He found the basket hanging on a nail by the door.

The chickens all stared at Dink as he approached their roosting places. "Good morning, you guys," Dink said in what he hoped was a soothing voice. "Got eggs?"

He reached out one hand slowly and slid it beneath a plump white hen. She cocked her head at him but didn't seem to mind his hand. Dink's fingers found two warm eggs.

Grinning, he set them in the basket and moved to the next nest. Five minutes later, he walked into the kitchen with sixteen eggs.

"Ah, enough for pancakes," Mario said. "You feel like being my assistant? Grab that apron off the hook."

"Awesome!" Dink said, tying a large white apron around his waist. It reached to the tops of his sneakers.

They worked together for a while, then Mario thanked Dink and sent him back to Moose Cabin.

"I appreciate your help," the cook said. "You'll make a great chef someday!"

Dink smiled and headed back toward the cabins. The sun was glinting through the trees now, turning the dewy lawn into a blanket of tiny diamonds.

The guys in Moose Cabin were tumbling out of bed, searching for something to wear. Dink grabbed his toothbrush and headed for the washhouse.

Josh was already there, and Dink told him what he'd been doing.

"You got to make pancakes?" Josh said with toothpaste foam on his lips. "And you let me sleep?"

"All I did was crack eggs and throw stuff in a big bowl," Dink said. Then he grinned. "Mario did say he thought that I'd make an excellent chef!"

Josh shook his head. "I'll bet there'll be eggshells in all the pancakes," he said.

"Nope," Dink said, turning on the water. "Just in yours."

At eight o'clock, everyone was sitting at the picnic tables. Dink and Josh waved at Ruth Rose, and she joined them at their table.

"I snuck back in the lodge this morning," Dink whispered. "The ring

was still there. I hope she finds it."

"Who's that guy?" asked Josh, pointing toward a man talking with Buzzy.

The man had sleek gray hair. He was thin, had a pointy nose, and was dressed in a gray tracksuit. He reminded Dink of a greyhound dog. His small black eyes seemed to take in everything.

The man sat down at another table, and Buzzy walked into the kitchen. He and the other counselors brought out

platters of pancakes, jugs of syrup, and pitchers of orange juice.

"Guys, I just thought of something," Ruth Rose said. "I want to find out if Mademoiselle Musée found her ring yet. Want to come and see her with me?"

"When?" Josh asked.

"Now, right after we eat," Ruth Rose said. "It'll just take a minute."

After a few minutes, Luke blew his whistle. "Good morning, everyone!" he said. "I hope you all slept well. How about a big cheer for Mario's fabulous flapjacks!"

Everyone clapped and whistled.

"And this gentleman is Detective Robb," Luke went on. "He's going to be your teacher this week. You'll learn all about fingerprinting and other cool stuff. Mademoiselle Musée has agreed to teach you about forgery. It's gonna be a great week!"

The man in gray stood up and nodded his head. "Morning, kids," he said. "Don't let me interrupt your breakfast. Dig in!"

"One more thing," Angie called out. "Everyone come back here right after chores. You'll get your map clues and you can start to hunt for the treasure!"

Everyone cheered, then started to eat.

Dink, Josh, and Ruth Rose finished first, then got up and headed for the kitchen.

"How were those flapjacks?" Mario asked, winking at Dink.

"The best I ever ate," Josh said, "even if Dink's hands touched the batter!"

The kids entered the dining room. Mademoiselle Musée was standing at the table with her back to them.

"Um, excuse me," Ruth Rose said.

Mademoiselle Musée turned around.

Dink looked past her at the box of latex gloves. The ring was gone. *Good,* he thought.

"We wondered if you found your ring," Ruth Rose asked.

The woman stared at the three kids. "Yes, I found it here this morning," she said. "I—I must have forgotten where I put it."

"Great!" Ruth Rose said. "You said you might show us how you clean paintings, so we . . ."

"Yes," the woman said. "Come closer, but please touch nothing." The kids gathered around her.

The painting was still there. Dink could see a barn, children playing in the snow, and the yellow house with smoke coming from the chimney, all under a bright blue sky.

Mademoiselle Musée pulled off her gloves, dropped them into a basket under

the table, then pulled a fresh pair on.

"I have finished this painting," she said, sliding it to the center of the table. "But I will demonstrate on one that I have not yet cleaned."

She walked quickly into the great room and returned with a painting only as large as a book. Flipping the small painting over, she pulled out a few nails with pliers. She slid the canvas out of the frame and laid it on the table.

The kids looked at the soiled painting. It was impossible to tell what was beneath the dirt.

Mademoiselle Musée picked up a cotton ball and wet it from one of the bottles. "As you can see, this painting is covered with years of soot and smoke," she said. Moving her hand in a small circle, she began gently wiping the damp cotton ball over a small section of the painting. Slowly the dirt disappeared until the green branches of a tree became visible.

"That's amazing!" Ruth Rose said. "Who painted this?"

"I won't know until I clean the entire painting," Mademoiselle Musée said.

Then she pointed to the winter-snow scene. "But that one is a Grandma Moses."

"Who's she?" asked Josh.

"My grandmother loves her paintings!" Ruth Rose said. "She was real old when she painted, right, Mademoiselle Musée?"

"Yes, she started out as a simple farmer's wife," Mademoiselle Musée said, "and now some of her paintings are worth millions of dollars."

CHAPTER 7

"M-millions?" Josh said.

Mademoiselle Musée nodded at him. "Grandma Moses was becoming well known before she died," she said. "Now that she's been dead for years, she's very famous!"

"How come she painted on wood instead of canvas?" Dink asked. He pointed to the smoothly cut edges of the Grandma Moses painting.

"That is not wood," Mademoiselle Musée said. "Grandma Moses lived in the country and could not buy artist canvases. But she had fiberboard in her barn, so she often used that. It is thin, but very hard."

"How long does it take you to clean a painting?" Josh asked.

"Perhaps two days for one this size," Mademoiselle Musée answered. "Longer if I have to make repairs."

"How do you do that?" Dink asked.

"The canvas can become cracked or even ripped," Mademoiselle Musée explained. "Or when it's on fiberboard, the paint sometimes flakes off. I make the repairs, then paint over the damaged places."

"Guys, we'd better get back to our cabins," Ruth Rose said. "Thanks a lot, Mademoiselle Musée!"

"It is nothing," the woman said.

The kids hurried out of the lodge and ran toward the cabins. "It's time for chores," Ruth Rose said. "I'll see you later, okay?"

The guys nodded and walked to their own cabin. They found Buzzy taping a paper on the door, next to the schedule.

"Hi, guys," he said. "This is a chore list. All eight of you have to pitch in, but it shouldn't take more than fifteen minutes."

Dink and Josh read the list. Next to Josh's name they read SWEEP FRONT PORCH. Dink saw that his job was to straighten up the books and games shelf.

"Where are the brooms?" Josh asked Buzzy.

"In the closet inside the washhouse," Buzzy told him. Josh hiked over while Dink began organizing the games and books. The other six boys were sweeping, dusting, smoothing out sleeping bags, and straightening their cubbies.

Ten minutes later, everyone was finished. "Super job, you guys," Buzzy said. He looked at his watch. "It's time to head back to the lodge for your clues to find the mystery map!"

They all ran to the picnic tables. When everyone was there, Angie stood on a bench and held up a paper bag.

"We've already hidden the twenty-six map pieces," she said. "Now you can pick your clue cards that will help you find them."

She walked around and let each kid put a hand in the bag and pull out a card.

Dink's card had a big *B* written on the front. He turned the card over and found a feather taped there.

"What did you get?" Dink asked Josh and Ruth Rose, showing them his card.

"I have a *G,*" Ruth Rose said. "With a flower petal on the back."

"Mine is *M,*" Josh said. He flipped the card over and found some brownish hairs taped in place.

"Okay, everyone has a card now," Angie called out. "The letter is one clue, and the item on the back is a second clue. Have fun!"

"This is so cool," Ruth Rose said. "But I think mine is too easy. *G* must stand for *garden.*"

"Yeah, but which garden?" Dink asked. "There are flowers planted everywhere!"

Dink took another look at his card and the feather on the back. "What do you guys think?" he asked.

"Easy," Josh said. *"Birdbath."*

"It could also be *birdhouse* or *bird-feeder,*" Ruth Rose said. "Whose clue should we do first?"

"Mine," Dink said.

"Why you?" Josh asked.

"Because these are alphabet clues, and *Dink* comes before *Josh* and *Ruth Rose* in the alphabet!" Dink announced.

"Okay, let's go see where the birds hang out," Ruth Rose said.

The kids walked around the lodge. They waved to other kids wandering around with white cards in their hands.

They found a hummingbird feeder, but saw no ripped piece of map.

They peeked inside a birdhouse, but saw only twigs and dead grass.

"Look," Josh said. He pointed to a few birds splashing in a birdbath.

The kids rushed over, scaring the

birds into a nearby tree. The birdbath was made of a concrete bowl standing on a pedestal.

"I don't see a piece of map," Josh said.

Dink tipped the water out and removed the bowl. Underneath, stuck there with masking tape, was a piece of paper. "I found it!" he cried.

They all looked at the fragment of paper. Its edges were torn on all sides but one. That side had a dark blue line. Some pencil lines had been drawn on the paper, but they made no sense.

"One down, twenty-five to go," Dink said.

"Let's look for a garden," Ruth Rose said, glancing at her own card.

"Wait a sec," Josh said. He found a hose attached to the lodge and filled the birdbath with clean water.

The kids roamed around the lodge, checking out flower beds. They saw plenty of flowers, but no map pieces.

Ruth Rose studied the petal that was taped to the back of her card. She smelled it and rubbed her finger across its surface. "This looks like some of my grandmother's roses," she said. "Let's look for roses."

On the south side of the lodge, in full

sunlight now, stood three rosebushes. Each held several pink blossoms. Ruth Rose compared the living blooms to the petal on her card. "I can't tell if they're the same," she said. "This petal is drying up."

There was a ring of smooth rocks surrounding the small garden. Ruth Rose began looking under each rock. She found the map piece under the last one.

The kids stared at the piece of paper in Ruth Rose's hand. It was the same kind of paper Dink had found under the birdbath. This piece had four letters written on it in block letters.

"*E-T* and *F-R*," Josh said. "They must be parts of words."

"I wonder if the other kids are finding their pieces," Dink said, looking around. Kids were all over the camp, each one carrying a card.

"Let's look for yours now, Josh," Ruth Rose said.

They studied the hairs that were taped on his card.

"*M* could stand for a lot of things," Josh said. "Like *marshmallow.*"

"Marshmallows don't have hair," Ruth Rose reminded him.

"Duh," Josh said.

"Do you think these are human hairs?" Dink asked. "Oh my gosh, they could be from Mario's mustache!"

"Or Mademoiselle Musée's hair!" Ruth Rose said.

"No," Josh said. "These hairs are light brown with a little white. She has black hair, and Mario's mustache is very dark brown."

"They could be bristles from some kind of brush," Dink said.

"I saw a lot of paint cans in the barn, and there are a bunch of brushes hanging on the wall," Ruth Rose said. "We could try there."

"But what about this *M*?" Josh asked, tapping his card.

"Maybe the brushes have labels," Dink suggested. "We might find an *M* on a label."

"It's worth a look," Josh said. The kids ran to the barn and peered in. A few other kids were in there, searching through stuff.

"Any luck?" one of Ruth Rose's cabinmates asked.

"We found two," Ruth Rose said.

"Cool!" the girl answered. "Some of the boys in Bear Cabin have found four already!"

Josh stood on a box and examined the row of upside-down paintbrushes. Some of the brush handles had labels, but none of the labels had an *M*. And the hairs on his card didn't match any of the brush bristles.

"What about some other kind of brush?" Dink said, studying Josh's clue card. "My dad used to have a shaving brush made of badger hairs. I wonder if Mario uses one."

The kids raced to the kitchen. They found Mario stirring a big pot.

"How's your treasure hunt going?" he asked.

"We found two, but we're having a hard time with this one," Josh said. He showed Mario the *M* on his card and the hairs on the back.

"Um, do you have a shaving brush like this?" Dink asked.

Mario glanced at the card. "Nope. I use an electric razor," he said.

"Well, thanks anyway," Josh said.

The kids sat on the steps facing the barn.

"Guys, we're stupid!" Dink said all

of a sudden. "*M* is for *moose,* and there's a moose head over the fireplace in the dining room. I'll bet these are moose hairs!"

The kids raced through the kitchen and into the dining room. Mademoiselle Musée was gone. The small painting she had shown them was on the table, partly cleaned. Now they could see a row of trees and some clouds.

"How do I get up there to Mr. Moose?" Josh asked.

"I'll see if Mario has a stepladder," Ruth Rose said. She scampered back toward the kitchen.

There were framed photographs, vases, and other small objects on the mantel below the moose head. Josh began looking under or inside each one.

Dink peeked into the great room to see if Mademoiselle was there. She was not, but Dink noticed several framed paintings stacked on a sofa. He could only see the top one, a picture of some Native Americans walking along a path near a river. To Dink, the picture looked freshly cleaned. He assumed Mademoiselle Musée had put these here to be rehung on the walls of the great room.

"Got one," Ruth Rose said, carrying a metal stepladder over to Josh.

He climbed on it and held his card up to the hairs on the moose's face and beard.

"The color looks right, but the moose hairs are thicker than these," Josh said. He tugged a few hairs from the moose head.

He came down off the ladder. "See," he said, holding the moose hairs next to those on his card. "Mine are thinner."

"How about artist's paintbrushes?" Ruth Rose said. "Some of my grandmother's brushes have hairs that look like the ones on Josh's card."

"Maybe," Josh said. "And this *M* could stand for *Mademoiselle Musée.* She has some brushes in her trunk."

"Yeah, but she wouldn't want us messing with them," Dink said.

Josh walked over to Mademoiselle Musée's trunk, and Dink followed him. There were faded labels on the sides and top. One of the labels said PROPERTY OF MURN THE MAGICIAN.

"Who's Murn?" Josh asked.

"Maybe Mademoiselle Musée got the trunk from a magician," Dink said. "He could've kept all his magic stuff inside, like she does with her cleaning things."

The upright trunk was closed. On the left side, there were three latches that held the lid shut.

"Should we open it?" Ruth Rose asked, standing next to Josh. "We wouldn't touch anything, just look for the map piece, right?"

"I guess it wouldn't hurt anything to just take a quick peek," Dink said. "There's no lock on it."

Josh reached out and flipped the top latch. The lid stayed shut. He flipped the next latch down, and the lid swung open sideways, like a door. But instead of shelves holding jars and other supplies, the kids were looking at the Grandma Moses painting. There was a secret compartment inside the door of the trunk!

"What's *this* doing here?" Dink asked. "Why hasn't she hung it back on the wall?"

"There are more paintings behind this one," Josh said.

Dink counted five behind the Grandma Moses.

"Maybe she stores them in this hollow door until she's ready to frame them again," Ruth Rose suggested.

Dink reached out a finger and touched the paint on the Grandma Moses painting. It was dry. He ran his thumb along the edges of the fiberboard. They felt rough and bumpy.

A thought was trying to force its way out of Dink's brain. He knew it was important by the way his arms erupted into goose bumps. But before he could pin the thought down, he heard footsteps on the stairs.

"Mademoiselle Musée!" Ruth Rose mouthed.

Dink swung the trunk lid shut and flipped the latches back into place. "Let's go before she sees us," he whispered to Josh and Ruth Rose. They slipped through the dining room door and headed for their cabins.

CHAPTER 8

The kids jogged toward the trees behind Moose Cabin. When they came to the fence, they vaulted over it. Once they were in the woods, Dink stopped short.

"What's the matter?" Ruth Rose asked, catching her breath.

Josh flopped on the ground.

"Guys, I think Mademoiselle is stealing the paintings we saw in that secret compartment in her trunk!" Dink said.

"Stealing them?" Josh asked.

Dink nodded. "Can you think of another reason she'd have those paintings hidden inside the trunk like that?"

"Maybe she just doesn't want them lying around where anybody could see them," Ruth Rose said. "Especially that Grandma Moses, which is real valuable."

"Or she could be waiting till the paint is dry enough before she frames them," Josh put in.

Dink shook his head. "The paint is dry," he said. "I felt it."

Josh stood up and brushed pine needles from his knees. "Well, what should we do?"

"I don't know," Dink said. "But I'm going to keep my eye on her. *And* that trunk!"

Ruth Rose looked at her watch. "We have three minutes to get to the picnic tables," she said. "Detective Robb will be waiting for us."

"Maybe we should tell him about what we saw in the trunk," Josh said.

"I don't know," Dink said. "I could be wrong. Anyway, we'd better get over there."

The kids jogged to the picnic tables and found places to sit. Everyone else was there. Mademoiselle Musée was standing next to Detective Robb.

"So how many of you have followed your card clues and found the map piece?" Detective Robb asked.

Almost every hand went up. Only a couple of kids, including Josh, had not been successful yet.

"Okay, maybe you can find 'em later today," Detective Robb said.

He turned to Mademoiselle Musée. "In case you haven't met her yet, this is Mademoiselle Musée. She has a fascinating job. She cleans and restores old paintings," he said. "She lives in France, but was hired by the Darbys to come here and clean their paintings. She has seen thousands of signatures, and some of them have been forged, right, Mademoiselle?"

She bowed her head. "There are many clever forgers out there," she said.

"Will you tell the kids how you can tell the difference between a real signature and a forged one?" Detective Robb asked.

"Of course," she said. "There are four things to look for." Dink noticed that she was still wearing white latex gloves when she raised one finger.

"First, study the overall look of the signature," Mademoiselle Musée went on. "You may not be able to say exactly what it is, but there is something different about this signature."

She held up a second finger. "Next, the length of the signature. Each time we sign our name, our signature is almost exactly the same length. Try it sometime. But forged signatures are often shorter or longer than the actual signature."

She went on to describe how a forger will lift his pen off the paper as he studies the signature he's trying to copy. When the forger puts his pen back on the paper, he leaves a tiny space. Sometimes, she went on, there will be a space and a tiny ink blot if the forger is using a ballpoint pen.

Mademoiselle Musée held up her fourth finger. "Most forgers are nervous," she said with a little smile. "Their hand trembles as they are forging a name. Experts can spot signs of these hand tremors."

She told Detective Robb that she had work to do. The kids all clapped, and she disappeared into the house.

"How would you like to see if you can all pick out a forged signature?"

Detective Robb asked the kids.

"Cool!" one of the Bear Cabin boys said.

Detective Robb passed out a sheet of paper and a pencil to everyone. Each sheet was covered with signatures.

"In each row of three signatures, two are real and one is a forgery," Detective Robb said. "Circle the one you think is fake."

Dink glanced down at his paper. He saw *George Washington, Elvis Presley,* and a bunch of other famous names. He looked for spaces between letters and tiny blots of ink. In the George Washington row, he circled the one signature that was shorter than the other two.

After five minutes, Detective Robb asked the kids to stop. "Now I'd like you to try forging a signature. Pick any name on your paper and try to copy it exactly. I think you'll find it's pretty difficult."

Detective Robb walked around and looked at the kids' papers. "Say, that's an excellent replica of Abe Lincoln's signature," he said as he walked past Josh. "I'll bet you draw or paint, am I right?"

Josh nodded. "I like to draw a lot," he said.

"I thought so," Detective Robb said. "You'd make a good forger!"

"Hey, Josh, forge me a check for a million dollars!" Brendan called out.

Everyone laughed except Dink. He put his pencil down next to his paper. The thought that had been buzzing in his brain like a bee in a bottle finally surfaced.

"It's almost eleven-thirty," Detective Robb called out. "We have to stop now. Tomorrow I'll show you how to find and lift fingerprints."

"Don't leave yet," Dink said quietly to Josh and Ruth Rose.

The three of them stayed seated while the rest of the kids wandered toward the cabins. Detective Robb picked up his coffee mug and went into the kitchen.

Josh looked at Dink. "What's going on? You look like you sat on a tack."

"I figured out how Mademoiselle Musée is stealing the paintings," Dink said very quietly. "I think she's making copies of them and keeping the real ones."

Josh and Ruth Rose just stared at him.

"What do you mean? How do you know?" asked Ruth Rose.

"I can't prove it, but listen," Dink said. He started by telling Josh and Ruth Rose about the yellow paint he'd gotten on his pajama sleeve.

"When we snuck in to return the ring last night, I looked at the painting she left under the towel. I must have dragged my sleeve across it," Dink said. "The paint was still wet! We thought that was the real Grandma Moses painting. But I think it was a copy that Mademoiselle Musée painted. I think she hid the real one inside the hollow door on the trunk. We just saw it there!"

"So where's the copy?" Josh asked.

Dink remembered the stack of framed paintings on the sofa.

"I think it's in the great room, waiting to be hung on the wall," he said. "When the Darbys see it, they'll think it's the real one."

"They'd never even know the difference!" Ruth Rose said. "They'd just think she did an excellent job of cleaning it."

Dink nodded. "Remember how Mademoiselle Musée told us Grandma

Moses painted on fiberboard?" Dink asked. "Well, my dad uses fiberboard for projects. It's really hard stuff. He has to cut it with a power saw. The painting we saw under the towel had really smooth edges, like it was cut with a modern saw. But the painting inside the trunk door had rough edges. Like they were cut by an old person with a handsaw."

"What a scam!" Josh said. "I'll bet she looked up all the Darbys' paintings in that book of hers. When she found ones that were valuable, she made copies and hid the real ones in the trunk door!"

Detective Robb walked out of the kitchen with a fresh mug of coffee.

"You three look like you're up to something," he joked.

Dink made up his mind. "Detective Robb, can we tell you something?" he said. "It's, um, pretty bad."

The detective nodded and sat on the kids' bench. "Of course. What's bothering you?"

Dink repeated everything he, Josh, and Ruth Rose had talked about. When he got to the part about finding the paintings inside the hollow trunk door, Detective Robb raised his eyebrows.

"Have you told anyone else your suspicions?" he asked Dink.

Dink shook his head. He felt better now that he'd told someone, but his heartbeat was still racing.

"This is a serious accusation," the detective went on. "Still, I can see how it's possible. Mademoiselle Musée told me she was a painter first, then turned to art restoration. When she realized that the Darbys owned some valuable paintings, maybe she couldn't resist the chance to make some easy money."

"Do you think she was planning to sell the paintings she hid?" Josh asked.

Detective Robb nodded. "More than likely. There are plenty of art buyers who don't care where paintings have come from," he said, standing up. "Don't tell anyone else what we've talked about. I have to make a call and put some things in place. Then I'll have a talk with Mademoiselle Musée."

Detective Robb looked down at the kids. "And stay out of the lodge," he said.

CHAPTER 9

The kids watched Detective Robb pull out a cell phone as he walked away.

"This is creepy," Josh said. "Should we go back to the cabin?"

"We eat lunch in fifteen minutes," Dink said. "We might as well wait here."

Just then Remote the goat and Ronald the rooster came around the corner of the barn. Remote headed right for the kids, but Ronald stopped to scratch in the dirt.

The goat rested his chin on Josh's knee.

"My dog does that when he wants to

be scratched," Josh said, stroking the goat's silky ears.

"Oh my gosh!" Ruth Rose cried, making the goat back up. "Josh, your *M* stands for *Mote!*"

"*M-O-A-T,* like surrounding a castle?" Josh asked.

"No, *Mote* is Buzzy's nickname for Remote, remember?" she said. "And Buzzy made up some of these clue cards. So maybe the *M* stands for *Mote,* and those are goat hairs on your card!"

"Ruth Rose, you're a genius!" Josh said. He pulled out his clue card and compared the hairs on the back to the goat's hairs.

"They're the same!" Dink said.

"So do you think the map piece is hidden on Mote?" Josh asked.

"Luke said the clues would lead us to a place," Ruth Rose said. "Where's Mote's place?"

"I know!" Dink said, bolting toward the barn. He showed Josh and Ruth Rose the doghouse where the goat slept. "I'll bet the map piece is in there."

Josh got down on his knees and peered through the opening. "I hope he didn't eat it," he said, crawling inside.

Josh began turning over the straw bedding. After a minute, he backed out holding a flat tin box. "Ta-da!"

Josh opened the box and found a piece of paper that looked like the ones Dink and Ruth Rose had found.

"We found it!" Ruth Rose said.

"Just in time for lunch," Josh said, grinning.

The kids ran around to the picnic tables. Most of the other campers were there, but a few stragglers were just arriving.

Dink, Josh, and Ruth Rose sat together just as Buzzy, Luke, and Angie came out through the kitchen door. Buzzy stood on a bench and blew his whistle.

"Detective Robb is busy, but he wanted us to ask if anyone is still missing his or her map piece," the tall teenager said.

No hands went up.

"That's awesome!" Buzzy said.

Luke went around and collected all twenty-six map pieces.

"Now, since there are so many of you, each cabin should select one person," Buzzy went on, "and those three kids will meet and assemble the map."

"Why can't we all do it together?" one girl asked.

Angie laughed. "Have you ever tried to put a jigsaw puzzle together with twenty-five other kids helping? That's two hundred sixty fingers altogether!"

Everyone laughed.

"Can they put the map together right now?" Duke asked.

"Sure," Luke said. "The three you choose can work on it while we eat lunch. So get in a huddle with your cabinmates and vote for who you think would do a good job on the map."

The kids scrambled around and formed into three groups by cabin.

"I nominate Dink," Josh said to the rest of his group. "He's really good at puzzles and stuff."

Dink was chosen.

A minute later, he found himself sitting with Jade from Fox Cabin and Stanley from Bear Cabin. Luke came over and piled the map pieces on the table in front of them. "I'll give you a hint," Luke whispered. "The edges have a dark blue line."

The three kids went to work. Many of the pieces had blue lines, so it took only a minute to assemble the four edges. Then they worked on the inside. As the map took shape, the kids saw a picture of the lake, the dock, and the ring of stones around the campfire. There was a big *X* drawn at one spot, on a flat rock. An arrow pointed from the dock to the *X*. Dink realized that the ET and FR he'd seen on Ruth Rose's map piece were part of a sentence: MEASURE TEN FEET FROM THE DOCK.

"The treasure must be under that rock!" Stanley said.

Just then the three counselors came over to their table. "Guys, your lunch is waiting," Buzzy said. "How're you doing with the map?"

"We finished!" Jade said.

"You guys are amazing!" Angie said. "Now go back to your tables and tell the other kids what you learned. After lunch, you can all run down to the lake

and get your well-earned treasure."

Mario had heaped platters with rolls, cheese and tomato slices, and three kinds of sandwich meat. The kids built their own sandwiches. They gulped them down with milk, then took off for the lake.

The fastest runners were already moving the rock when Dink, Josh, and Ruth Rose got there. Everyone gathered around as Jade began digging in the sand under the rock.

A minute later, she held up a plastic baggie. Inside was a folded sheet of paper. Jade unzipped the baggie and read the note: *"Congratulations! Your treasure is a lobster feast tonight. Come here at five o'clock, and wear your bathing suits!"*

The note was signed by Angie, Buzzy, and Luke.

"Lobsters! Awesome!" Josh said.

Angie and Luke had walked up behind the group.

"Good work, kids," Angie said. "Now it's time to head back to your cabins for a while. At one-thirty, meet at the barn to choose an activity. Luke will take some of you canoeing if you choose that. I'll be with the kids who want archery or crafts."

"Where's Buzzy?" Campbell asked.

"He's . . . he's busy," Angie said. "Okay, we'll see you all later."

The kids started to head toward the path. Angie stopped Dink, Josh, and Ruth Rose. "They want you three in the lodge," she said quietly.

"Who does?" Dink asked.

"The Darbys," she answered. "And Detective Robb." Then she followed the rest of the kids toward the cabins.

CHAPTER 10

Dink had eaten too fast. Now his stomach felt like he'd swallowed marbles. "What if Mademoiselle Musée is there?" he asked. "What if I was all wrong, and she's going to sue me or something?"

"Let's just go and find out," Josh said. "And if you go to jail for breaking and entering her trunk, I'll bring you a lobster claw."

Dink, Josh, and Ruth Rose walked toward the lodge. The first thing they saw was a police cruiser parked in front of the porch.

"They must be here to arrest Mademoiselle Musée!" Ruth Rose whispered.

"Or Dink," Josh teased.

Dink found that his mouth was too dry to say anything back to Josh.

The front door of the lodge opened. Two police officers escorted Mademoiselle Musée out of the building and down onto the driveway. Her hands were handcuffed in front of her.

With Mademoiselle Musée in the

backseat of the cruiser, the officers drove away.

Detective Robb held the door open for the kids. "Come on in," he said. "The Darbys are waiting for you." He led them into the great room.

Michael and Bessie Darby were sitting on one of the sofas. Sitting between them and holding Bessie's hand was Buzzy Steele.

"Well, hello," Michael Darby said when he saw the kids enter. "Please sit. Mario is going to bring us all some lemonade."

The kids sat on another sofa facing the Darbys and Buzzy.

Buzzy looked at Dink, Josh, and Ruth Rose. He winked.

"First I want to thank you three for exposing Mademoiselle Musée for the thief she is," Michael Darby said. "When we decided to open this little camp, we

had no idea any *real* detective work would be necessary!"

"Mademoiselle Musée admitted to everything," Detective Robb told the kids. "If you three hadn't figured out what she was up to, she'd have walked out of here with several extremely valuable paintings."

Bessie Darby turned to Buzzy. "Dear, why don't you tell the children the rest of the story?"

Buzzy blushed. "Okay, Grandma," he said.

"You're the Darbys' grandson?" Josh blurted out.

"Yep, I sure am," Buzzy said. "I didn't say anything because I wanted all the kids to treat me the same as Luke and Angie. Anyway, this is what happened. When Mademoiselle Musée came—"

"By the way, her real name is Maude

Murn," Detective Robb said. "She wasn't from France at all. But she's wanted in five states out west. In Arizona, she's known as Maude the Fraud. She left there in a hurry and changed her name when she got here."

"When she got here to clean the paintings, my grandparents told her about Detective Camp and all the kids we were expecting," Buzzy said. "I guess she figured with a detective and a bunch of kids snooping around, her scam might be discovered. So she made a plan, right, Detective Robb?"

He nodded. "She decided to add some confusion so no one would pay her any attention," Detective Robb said. "She took a few pieces of the Darbys' silver and hid them under mattresses in the kids' cabins. Then she went to the Darbys and told them she'd seen a kid running out of the great room. The

Darbys warned Buzzy about it."

"My grandparents asked me to search the cabins," Buzzy continued. "I did, and found the silver animals. I put them in my trunk for safekeeping." He blushed again. "I admit, I thought some of the kids had stolen the silver."

"Then Maude pretended her ring had been stolen and hid it under a mattress," Detective Robb went on. "She planned to demand a search. She figured the 'stolen' stuff would be found, kids would be accused, and the Darbys would send you all home. Then she could continue with her scam. But Ruth Rose found the ring before Maude could get a search going."

"So her plan to shut down the camp backfired," Michael Darby said. "Thank goodness you clever kids discovered her trunk's secret hiding place!"

"Turns out her father was a magician, and that was his trunk," Detective Robb said. "He used to hide things inside that hollow door."

Bessie Darby sighed. "So sad. The woman was a talented painter and restorer, but she threw it all away because she was greedy."

"What will happen to her?" Ruth Rose asked.

"She'll go back to Arizona for trial," Detective Robb said. "Thanks to you three awesome detectives!"

At five o'clock, everyone feasted on lobster, corn on the cob, salad, and ice cream. The Darbys came to the lake and sat in lawn chairs out of the sun. At six o'clock, Buzzy supervised swimming and diving off the dock. Some kids went canoeing with Angie and Luke.

Dink, Josh, and Ruth Rose were standing up to their shoulders in the clear, still-warm lake water.

"I wonder if that monster really is hibernating in this lake," Josh said, peering down into the water.

"Maybe you're standing on him," Dink said. "Better watch out, Josh."

"I'm not afraid of any old monst—"

Suddenly Josh's eyes opened wide. His tongue drooped out of his mouth, he fell over, and he disappeared under the water.

"Josh the joker," Dink said.

"I wonder how long he'll stay under," Ruth Rose said, looking into the water where Josh had been standing.

Just then she let out a yell and jumped into the air. "Something pinched me!" she said. "It felt like a—"

Josh's laughing face broke the surface. He was holding a red lobster claw, making the two pincers open and close. "That's for scaring me last night, Ruth

Rose," he said. "Now we're even!"

"You're so immature," Ruth Rose said.

Then she jumped on Josh and dunked him under the water.

DID YOU FIND THE
SECRET MESSAGE
HIDDEN IN THIS BOOK?

If you *don't* want
to know the answer,
don't look at the bottom
of this page!

HAVE YOU READ ALL THE BOOKS IN THE

A TO Z Mysteries®

SERIES?

Help Dink, Josh, and Ruth Rose . . .

...solve
mysteries
from A to Z!

Collect clues with
Dink, Josh, and Ruth Rose
in their next exciting
adventure

MAYFLOWER TREASURE HUNT

Dink, Josh, and Ruth Rose dug faster and faster. Piles of sand grew around their knees. They uncovered all sorts of things that had gotten left behind over the years: empty bottles, a button, part of a comic book.

"Yuck!" Josh yelled suddenly.

Dink looked at what had made Josh's face turn white. It was about the size of a hamster and covered with rotted brown skin.

Dink used a stick to lift that thing out of the hole.

"OH MY GOSH!" Ruth Rose yelled.

It was a decayed leather bag. As it fell away, something still hung from Dink's stick.

It was a necklace.

"The *Mayflower* jewels!" Dink said.

A TO Z MYSTERIES® fans, check out Ron Roy's other great mystery series!

Capital Mysteries

#1: Who Cloned the President?
#2: Kidnapped at the Capital
#3: The Skeleton in the Smithsonian
#4: A Spy in the White House
#5: Who Broke Lincoln's Thumb?
#6: Fireworks at the FBI
#7: Trouble at the Treasury
#8: Mystery at the Washington Monument
#9: A Thief at the National Zoo
#10: The Election-Day Disaster
#11: The Secret at Jefferson's Mansion
#12: The Ghost at Camp David
#13: Trapped on the D.C. Train!
#14: Turkey Trouble on the National Mall

January Joker
February Friend
March Mischief
April Adventure
May Magic
June Jam
July Jitters
August Acrobat
September Sneakers
October Ogre
November Night
December Dog
New Year's Eve Thieves

If you like **A to Z Mysteries**®,
take a swing at

BALLPARK Mysteries®

#1: The Fenway Foul-Up

#2: The Pinstripe Ghost

#3: The L.A. Dodger

#4: The Astro Outlaw

#5: The All-Star Joker

#6: The Wrigley Riddle

#7: The San Francisco Splash

#8: The Missing Marlin

#9: The Philly Fake

#10: The Rookie Blue Jay

#11: The Tiger Troubles

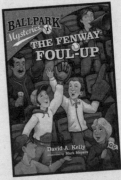